Awakenings 11:
Everything is Symbol

Kf.w M Kht

ISBN: 979-8-9887604-3-6

Dedicated to all Nstr.w and Gwnstr.w.
I endeavor always to make you proud I
am one of you.

And to my children whom I miss
dearly.

KUKIRI

Knowledge is useless that has not undergone rigorous debate, examination, scrutiny, and testing. It is merely gibber-jabber akin to preverbal, primate growls. The only way to ascertain whether knowledge contains Truth is to present it before those who will not only doubt its veracity but will also attack it mercilessly.

Figure 1 Rk M Kfw

Table of Contents

*I thought it was just a
series of random and
unrelated dreams. I could
not have been more wrong.
My god! I could not have
been more wrong.*

errazarre bizatic!)

Every bloom of dream
   plucks
        from real
herethen nowthere petals- strange
   pollinations of
      haphazard mind

Emerging as Seem
        fanciful thoughts-
flitterfluttering, bizzbuzzingly flightful,
weave surreal, honeycombed
              sin)ern patt(anes!
 enigmas
      separate yetconnected figments
of sublime Truth

After pausing a moment, I make a 180* turn. I close my eyes and allow St.w, Kf.w, and Mkht.w to enter me when they are ready. When they have accepted me, I kneel. I perform the ritual of The Three Taps.[1] Once I see ymyw.h't[2] have accepted my invitation and have gathered, I look over my right shoulder. There, I see i am sleeping. My Mother approaches my bed. She ensures my comfort, tucking me within Blankets of Time. I feel the warmth of Her love as She makes the final tuck and kisses me gently on the forehead. She smiles and lets Her hand linger on my face for a moment before She turns to Me and says, "There will be no need to rush, my son, explore. Time for you no longer exists. Witness. Learn." She smiles broadly. She embraces Me warmly.

She speaks:

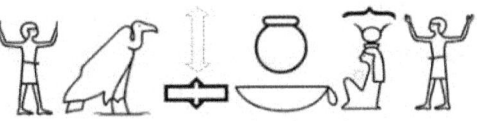

Figure 2 I am your mother (Y ynk mwt)

"who fashioned Your soul at the beginnings and ends. I am with You as you for this journey." She then melts into Me.

---

[1] Tap One: Informs the Ancestors an event is about to begin; Tap Two: Informs them in which direction to come; Tap three: Offers the invitation for them to join.
[2] The Ancestors

I lift my head to observe ymyw.h't who have gathered before me. There, kneeling directly in front of me, My Father. "Dad?" I say hesitantly. He smiles and says, "I am sure of it."

My Father speaks:

"One attains Sr.w[3] by navigating Dw.t[4]. The mysteries reveal this. You have discovered the cyclic nature of Sr.w attainment- The Diurnal Evaluations. Yet what you do not yet Rk[5] is the cyclic commencement. This begins during the Periods of Gestation during which HtHr.w[6] fashions the soul in Jmnt.j[7]. As it flows down Ytr.w[8] from Upper to Lower Km.t, navigating the cataracts, $\sqcup$[9] acquires the first of its Double Truths and becomes the Perpetual Initiate.

"During $\{ \bar{\circ} \}$[10] the Perpetual Initiate finalizes its journey by entering the Delta and passing through the First Portal; it resurrects the Father in the form of the Falcon, receives the Breath of Life and becomes upon the horizon. It is therefore extremely important that you understand: it is only by

---

[3] "Asaur"
[4] Duat or "netherworld"
[5] Know, have knowledge of
[6] "Hathor"
[7] "Amenta" or the "netherworld"
[8] Nile River
[9] K' or soul
[10] H'py- inundation

finding and fertilizing the ◡11 can man achieve immortality.

"Now, my son, it is time for you to become the second of your Double Truths." He then places his hand behind My neck. He leans toward me until our foreheads touch. He melts within me.

I stand. I stand before ymyw.h't. I look down over my right shoulder at sleeping me. "The butterfly, in order to be truly butterfly, must lose all notions of caterpillar."

I understand this me. he is symbol; he signifies a finite point within infinite pointlessness. To understand Me, I must understand his limitations- the confines of Space and Time within which he exists (his causes and effects). Only then can I understand Me as existence beyond those limits. Beyond time; beyond space. he is the symbol which bridges gaps between Me and my Ka as pattern manifest within potential (The First Double Truth). I smile. he will sleep as I explore- as I explore the infinite spatial and temporal me's into which ⊔ has coalesced. Perhaps, as I journey, he may come to understand he is one point along an infinite arc of Cycles and Rhythms. Beginnings and Ends. Livings and Dyings.

I turn toward ymyw.h't. They extend as far as I am, lining each side of my existence. I approach and face my grandfather. "Pop," I say to Him, "I commit to you at this moment, I will find the words." He smiles. He embraces and enters me. I turn to face and approach my grandmother. We embrace; "Of all gathered here," I

---

11 Sacred land

whisper in Her ear, "Nanna, I wish I could hold this embrace with you for all eternity." I feel the curl of Her lips on my neck as She smiles. "I told you," She says lovingly, "I am not There yet. I persist within you!" She then melts within me. I feel Her warmth. I face my grandfather, William Johnson. His smile is wide and beautiful. His eyes, blue and full of wisdom. "I have missed you dearly granddad," I say. "I am sorr..." He interrupts my apology by shaking His head "No." He simply stares into my eyes with empathy and compassion. "Out There, we are all victims of our environments," He says. He embraces and melts within me.

I move toward my grandmother, Aline Farmer. She inspects me knowingly. She smiles. "No words for now," She says, "we will speak at length later in your journeys." She embraces and melts into me.

I turn and stand between the expanse of ymyw.h't lining either side of me and extending into p't nn.w p't[12]. They stare into me with an intensity I have never experienced. They kneel and bow Their heads. Then They begin to speak. It is overwhelming. Their words spew forth in the manner of an excited child, eager to express a series of experiences it has had all at once, with no breaks, no pauses, no breaths. Their words emanate from every reality and SpaceTime with which Their consciousnesses have ever interacted- from within everywhere and everywhen They have existed:

---

[12] Beginnings of beginnings

In the beginning, Jtmn.nnw[13] of everything- and Bjn.bjn[14] vibrations. Now the formless rise and empty before speaks these first powerful Md.w, "darkness was surface of the deep, and Spirit was nothingness." Back there is this name: Time! Gracious, Merciful. Praise we to give this Lord of the Spaces. Master of Perpetual Nows. It is worship, and we beckon: guide us to the straight path. The path of those created in blessed totalities, not of those for whom there is division, nor of those who are in misguided heavens. The spirit of creation manifests first as the word spoken, which vibrates this consciousness into existence, and then Us. NTR creates Itself, then the others (perhaps "gods and demons,"), and finally T'Mry[15] by speaking its Md.w- revealing awareness of itself as themselves within; thus, creation exists as different aspects or "faces." Immediately, the All of All and primordial chaos still the process of separation; This promises eternity to the dead who are not yet born. The dead entreat: 𓀀𓁐𓏏𓂝𓏤𓈖𓏏[16] "do not pass us by; do not exclude us." In that same moment, Wpw.t, "opener of ways," allots to each of them a destiny within Rt.w[17] and holds all these fates in readiness to travel with You as you.

---

13 AtumNn.w prior to self-creation
14 Primordial mound of creation
15 Beloved land, i.e. Km.t
16 To those walking upon the Earth
17 Earth

Ymyw.h't raise Their heads and rise. Slowly and simultaneously- but nearly imperceptibly- They enter and melt within Me... as me.

Figure 3 Standing before ymyw.h't

Justice

I awaken within someone's dominant reality. I experience this reality through him. He is part of a small group of people, scantily dressed, who seem to me to be escapees from the institution of Early American Human Trafficking (part of the Underground Railroad perhaps?). The leader of this group resembles Denel Washington, but his name is John Brown. Based on conversations between them, I am within his brother Orville Brown. The group numbers approximately 30 people- men and women (I don't recall any children).

Figure 4 Justice

We are in a clearing within a forest. We walk single file. Suddenly, a member of the group, who is running point, halts us. Everyone drops to their knees, silently. We hear screaming in the distance; men, women, and children beaten and tortured. John immediately wants to render assistance. It is at this point I notice our group is armed. Heavily. I (Orville) tell John, we cannot go. We have to continue on our path. But John is insistent. I know, based on Orville's memories of their respect for John, this group will follow him to the depths of hell and battle satan himself if he commanded.

I take John's face into my hands. I say, "We are going to witness and hear terrible things John, horrible things. We have to keep our eyes focused on the war. That- over there- is a single battle. We have to know what battles to fight and which ones not to, as hard as that will be, if we are going to win this war against these devils. Do you understand me, John? He stares into my eyes. Tears flow down his face with Congo River intensity. He is transfixed. In the background, over my shoulder, the screaming and torture intensifies. John tries pushing past me when I hear noise coming from the rear- members of the group readying their weapons. They are fierce and fearless.

In the darkness we cannot be seen by a group of 3 men dragging a hand cuffed man along the forest. We only see silhouettes, but it is clearly a man dragged by a rope around his neck. I hear him struggling to breathe; I hear his body flailing along the ground. It is all I can do to restrain John. I have to place the entire weight of my body on him and cover his mouth. He is enraged.

After the men pass, we wait a few minutes in silence. When we are confident no one else is coming, we notice a larger silence of the forest. The torture has stopped. All we hear is the faint sound of fire crackle. We come to our knees and take quick count of our group. There are thirty of us. (In the system we use, everyone is assigned a number. You don't sound off on your number until you hear the person whose number is before you sound off theirs. This way, we can quickly know who is missing.) Everyone is accounted for.

John orders everyone to take account of themselves and drink some water. He is angry with me. I am angry with him. Though he is an excellent leader, he is impulsive. "What," I say to him in the darkness, "is your name?"

You know my name.

What is your name?

John Brown.

And who named you this?

Our mother.

And Why?

Because he fought to free us.

Yes, he fought, but he was impulsive, and that got him and all of his men killed. In the end, who did he free?

No one.

John, you have to think. You have to know when and when not to fight.

He is silent. Then he tells Orville to send 10 people to the area of the torture. It will be their job to scavenge whatever they can and report back on the scene they witness. It is always the same group of 10. Our best and most stealthy fighters. The rest of us gather in a circle and discuss our plans for the rest of the night. We decide we will travel to the outer edge of the nearest town, where we will scavenge for food and water while the town is sleep. That is how we move.

Sometime later, the scouting group reports back the settlement of blacks was completely burned, everyone was either killed or left for dead. "And those who suffered, who we could not save?" asked John. "We left, no one was suffering when we left boss," answered the leader of the party. (It is our way to kill those we cannot save or bring with us. We leave no one to suffer.) We took stock of and divided the scavenged materials between us. Then we let the scouting party rest before heading toward the nearest town.

As we move through the forest, we come across a man. He hangs from the branch of a large tree. His body slowly sways. Strange Fruit.

John orders us to cut him down. We bury him with honor and dignity.

In high grass, we make our way to the edge of a town. A woman bursts from a barn a short distance away. She is completely naked. Before the group can hide, she is upon us. She trips over someone's foot and lets out a loud, horrifying scream as she falls, "NOO!!! NO! PLEASE PLEASE!!!" One of the women of the group jumps on her and covers her mouth. The naked woman struggles violently. The woman of our group whispers something in her ear, and the woman instantly calms down, though breathing heavily.

Then, a man, apparently drunk, stumbles from the barn. He is yelling. He is looking for the naked woman. "Mary Benn, where you at, girl, where you get to little girl?" He stumbles such that though he is walking he makes no progress. He stops. He wobbles. "Where you at little girl; we not done playin, is we?" He laughs loudly.

John turns to the lady with Mary Benn. "Tell her to scream and say stay away from me." The lady whispers in Mary's ear. Mary shakes her head violently that she will not comply, but the woman of our group whispers in her ear

16

again. A very strange look comes over Mary's face. I see her eyes narrow. She is no longer afraid. A fierceness comes over her countenance. She takes a deep breath and yells, "Stay away from me," then she adds (I believe for the group's benefit), "and you and dem mens leave my baby alone in dat barn, Henrietta be only 11 years old. Leave her be, you devils!"

The drunken man, hearing Mary's voice, begins to stumble toward the hidden group. "C'mon girl, now we aint hurtin nothin, we jus having some fun. C'mon, lil girl." He reaches the edge of the group. He stops. Before he can utter a word or take another step, two of the scouts jump on him, knock him cold, and drag him into the tall grass. They drag him to Mary. They lay him next to her. She, for a moment, seems horrified, but the woman of the group whispers in her ear. Mary's entire demeanor changes. She kneels next to the man, who is beginning to wake. He tries to move, but two scouts have him pinned to the ground.

John quietly moves toward Mary. He hands her a machete. He doesn't say anything, but the look on his face tells her all. She takes the machete. She is hesitant. John says to her, "hurry, Mary, before they hurt your baby." With that, Mary plunges the machete into the man's abdomen. Then again, then again, then again, then… "save some for dem others," John says. Mary gathers herself. She stands, either no longer noticing or no longer caring she is naked. The scouts finish what Mary started.

I maneuver to the woman who whispered in Mary's ear. I ask her what she said that changed Mary's demeanor and heart. The woman takes two steps toward me. She stares deeply into my eyes for a very long time. She places her hand over my heart. She speaks:

"I say 'In 150 years, one of your children will come to this place wit us. He will tell what happened Here. Let 'm tell o ur bravery. Let 'm see how strong you are. He will need your strength to beat the devils O' his time. He Here now, watchin.'"

She takes two steps back, her eyes locked on mines. In the light of the moon, for the first time, I notice... Obsidian. She says, "Remember dis night, chile. When you go home, remember us, what happened. Do what we could not. Kill them all. Kill every last one O' dem."

In the barn, we hear the cries of a child and the drunken laughs of men. The group makes a way for Mary. "You lead us," John says to Mary. She makes a half-turn toward the group. She then turns toward the barn. She moves slowly, steadily. The group begins to advance with her, but John motions to the men to stand down. The women move as a single, determined unit. John turns to Orville. "Justice."

I exit that reality

TRAUMA IS AN EPIGENETIC INHERITANCE...AS IS TRIUMPH.

A Psychospiritual Occurrence

I am within this reality atop Columbia St. Mary's in Milwaukee. It is dark, ominous. Were my father not with me, I would be afraid. He and I watch children run across what seems to be oceans made of copper. They dance and play in its waves, but they are not happy. We are amazed the waves don't sever them in two. There are many people gathered, as though some sort of party. But everyone is somber- sad even. People cry as others throw themselves from the roof.

There is, however, one woman who seems saddest of all. She is beautiful. Stunning. She turns slightly toward my direction, and I see she is my ex-wife; but from which reality I cannot say.

I leave my father to approach and attempt conversation with her, but she is distant. She is on the verge of tears. I say to her, "At this moment, I can only offer a coupon." "A what?" she asks- confused. "Why? What can I do with a coupon?" "Redeem it when it has most value to you," I say calmly. "My coupon:

There are times
the events of which become
so harsh, so painful
we close ourselves
within
the darkest, loneliest parts

because
it is there, amidst the shadows,
pain seems most familiar
most comfortable
Most
Deserving.
where our screams become vocals
to which our dying dances
and our moans become hymns whose
 dreadful harmonies
 remind us
these pains are inevitable

I know these places
why people come, why you are... here

I cannot ask you to leave
I cannot offer solace
I can only promise
should you take hold of me
we will dance your sorrows
to seductive sambas
we will mend your wounds
til they wound round
rhythms that whisk us along windy walks
 through moonlit parks
 til your moans burst into
  carefree laughters
of old women
with so many coupons they know
their joys cost them
nothing

Figure 5 She Floated among the leaves

She then says, still hesitant: "A lovely sentiment, but how do I know you won't be gone by breakfast?"

"You don't," I reply, "just as trees don't know if or when will depart their leaves. That is hope, not knowing but remaining."

"How do you know I will remain if you leave?"

"That is **MY** hope."

I take her hand in mine; I lift it to my heart.

She draws me closer to her. She tilts her head upward. She holds me tight. She kisses me in ways I have never known. She whispers:

> *"I wish I could believe it is possible to be here, like this- forever. But sometimes, we simply cannot understand how it is we are so beautiful we could never be anything less than the most perfect of Autumn's leaves."*

She slowly draws away from me. Her beautiful obsidian eyes remain fixed on me as she slowly backs to and lets herself float from the edge of the roof to the pavement below.

She left me standing there with her love, or she left with mine.

She Exists Here

Figure 6 She exists here

I enter a reality sitting on the edge of a cliff with my daughter, Khabira. She is her current 12 years of age. We are looking to the skies, where we witness the merging of many and varied worlds. They merge in haphazard manners. There is no design to it. They merge, remain together for some time, separate, then merge with another. The process seems to repeat without end or meaning. My daughter doesn't seem particularly enthralled, although she is transfixed. It is as though her thoughts are someplace else. She frowns deep in thought.

"What is This, dad?" she asks.

"I think this is a dream," I reply.

Whose dream? Yours or mines?

I think it's my dream. This all seems familiar to me.

So, this is not real then?

I don't know if I can answer that yet. But it is a dream.

So, then you are asleep somewhere?

Yes.

Where?

My guess? At home.

So then where am I?

You are right Here sweetie.

No, dad, where am I in the world where you are sleeping and having this dream? Do I exist there?

Yes, you're my daughter. I guess you are in your room sleeping too.

So, I am not real right now?

What? Of course, you are. You are my daughter; I am your father.

No, dad. If I am asleep where you are sleep, I cannot be real, Here, in your dream because I am somewhere sleeping too. I can't be the real me in your dream AND the real me there. How can I be real in this dream AND real where I am asleep?

I don't know. But it may be possible in some kind of weird physics.[18]

But dad?

Yes sweetie?

Should I be able to remember what I did yesterday?

Of course, sweetie, why not?

No, dad, not the real me who is sleeping at home, the me Here right now. The one you are dreaming. Should I be

---

[18] Quantum Super Positioning(?)

able to remember what I did yesterday? Like, I remember having ice cream yesterday.

We didn't eat ice cream yesterday.

I did, dad. I ate ice cream yesterday. You were in your room, and I was eating ice cream. And dad?

Yes dear.

I can remember my whole life. How can I remember that if I am not real?

You are remembering what I remember. That's all.

But dad, you don't remember me eating ice cream yesterday, and I do. And dad?

Yes baby?

Can you tell me what else I did yesterday? Because I remember everything I did.

No sweetie, I can't.

WHY NOT? If I am in your dream, and your dream is in your head, EVERYTHING in your dream is in your head. That means my thoughts are in your head too. You should know what I am thinking, but you don't. WHY NOT?

I look over to her. She is not looking at me. She is deep in thought. I realize I have no idea what she is thinking. I think to myself, she is right, I SHOULD KNOW what she is thinking.

She slowly turns to me and says, "The thoughts I am thinking, dad, are not your thoughts. They are my thoughts. They are in my head. I am thinking them right now. They are not in your head. They are REAL thoughts. How can I be thinking REAL thoughts in someone else's dream? If I am not real right now, how can I be thinking REAL thoughts? And Dad?

Yes, Dear?

You are different.

Different? How am I different?

You don't seem like MY Dad.

What do you mean?

You are kinda the same, but you are different. I don't think you are MY dad. I think you are somebody else.

Who? Who do you think I am?

You are somebody else's dad.

Like my daughter who is asleep in my house?

No. Not her. YOU are not her dad either. HER dad is asleep in her house too. You are somebody else's dad.

Who?

I don't know, dad. I don't know, yet... Dad?

Yes, Tator?

Do you know somebody named Odjko?

The name sounds familiar, but I don't think so. Why?

I think that's who you are.

Odjko? No, sweetie, that's not who I am. I am...

Who? Who are you, dad. What is your name?

I... I don't... I am your dad.

No. Not MY DAD. But you are somebody's dad. I think your name is Odjko. I think that's who you are.

Why?

I don't know yet. But I think that's who you are... And dad?

Yes, baby?

I don't think you exist anymore.

What? But I am right here with you, sweetie.

No, no dad, you're not. I don't think you are anywhere.

Sweetheart, you are confusing me.

I know, dad, I know. And I'm sorry, but you shouldn't be Here.

Where should I be?

You shouldn't be anywhere dad. You shouldn't be anywhere.

She turns to me. Tears roll down her face. She experiences such sadness at this moment. "You don't exist, dad," she says. She hugs me. She whimpers. "I'm so sorry, dad," she

continues, "but this is not your dream. This is my dream. You're not my father. Your name is Odjko, and you don't exist. You used to, but something came and got you. It took you. You missed your granddaughter's birthday. She was sad. They miss you. But you don't exist anymore. You have to go."

I don't understand sweetheart.

Figure 7 My daughter explaining I don't exist

My dad, MY REAL dad, thought you didn't exist. He saw you and thought you were just part of a dream and that you didn't really exist. But you did. You were real, and... and dad?

Yes, baby?

I am so, so sorry. It was MY dad's fault. He didn't know, he didn't understand. You tried to tell him that time, remember? You tried to tell him you existed. You tried to tell him how to be Here. How to think when he's Here. But he didn't understand, and then you and that lady. He didn't think y'all were real. Remember?

Remember? Sweetie, I don't know what you are talking about.

I'm so, so sorry. It was MY dad's fault. He did that to you. But you have to go, dad. You shouldn't be Here. You shouldn't be anywhere.

That reality fades

Mr. Obama

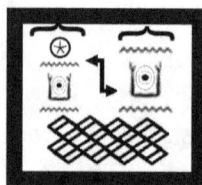

Figure 8 I combine my conscious reality with my dream reality

I enter a reality standing in a very large room filled with lots of people- men, women and children. It is some kind of gathering, a celebration? People laugh and converse everywhere. Some adults and I engage in play with water rifles. We are split into (teams?) of I don't know how many. Others seem to join at random. We dodge playfully, winding in and out of the adults and children present.

At one point, I am chasing someone when President Obama shows up. I almost drench him, but then pull back. He is amused, but he is also slightly annoyed that I did not include him. I tell him, "I don't want your secret service detail to pop out of nowhere and attack me." He laughs at this.

He and I are good friends. A friendship I fondly, briefly, and quickly reminisce over. It started before his term as Senator and when I was in the military.[19] I continue my play with the other adults, but I now also engage Mr. Obama in conversation.

---

[19] These memories are germane to this reality. In my dominant reality, I never knew- or even met- the president, and his presidency occurred long after I left the military in 1996. These memories of our friendship cover decades. The memories are extensive, vivid, and detailed. They are as real to me at this moment as any memories I have.

He talks to me about reading (or hearing about) the problems China is causing in the world. He says to me, "Who wants to consider these things when we are so close to thanksgiving?" He is really annoyed and bothered by the China thing. He waves to his wife, Michelle, who is in the distance speaking and laughing with other women and children.

I tell him I sent an email to his "people" requesting time with him so we can sit down and catch up on the progression of our lives since his presidency and my military days. He says to me, "since when have you ever needed an appointment, ole friend?" I point to his wife, and we both laugh loudly. Some adults attempt to splash him with water, but I and a group of others intervene, and he doesn't get wet. He laughingly says, "that's why you don't need an appointment, you keep me out of the hot and deep waters. BTW," he continues, "how is Ms. Mababu and the kids?" This sparks in me the brief visualization of a wife and kids. I am now married to Boy Mababu, who I met in the military. We are married, with 3 children, 2 boys and a girl. For some reason, I remember when we first met, when I met her brothers and father.

Mr. Obama laughs loudly then fades slowly away. I see his enormous and friendly smile. I pause briefly as my memories of him surface. I smile and lift my water rifle in salute to him. In the distance, I can see Mrs. Obama also fading from her group.

I and the other adults continue our play. At some point, I run out of water and need a refill. A group of men and women

Figure 9: I confuse my realities.

descend on me. They are about to drench me with water. Just then a group of three heavily armed Special Forces members materialize and kill the adults. Afterwards, one of the men (the leader?) turns to me and says, "Mr. Obama sends his regards." To which I, completely shocked (along with everyone else gathered), Exclaim, "Dude! We were just playing; these are water guns!!"

"Oh, my bad," he says nonchalantly, then kills one more male adult who was sneaking up behind me.

I exit that reality slightly pissed.

I think to myself: I live entire lives within these realities. The memories of and feelings for my (non-dominant) families and friendships begin to force themselves into my dominant consciousness. I am convinced, as I age and my mind becomes less plastic, I will fuse these realities into one memory.

An Overwhelming Sadness

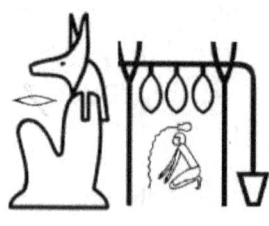

Figure 10 Overwhelming sadness

I enter this home within a non-dominant reality, but it is not the home in which I offer this rendering. It is of prior realities, many, many years ago. I have memories of this home, things I did while here, the people I encountered.

I sit in an upstairs room at the far end of the house. I think about the house. I reminisce about my past Here. My story within this house.

And then there is noise. Downstairs. Voices. Voices of children, happy and energetic. I hear them call out, "Dad, dad, where are you?" Their happiness is contagious and fills me with joy. "I am Here, you, guys, upstairs." The sound of scampering feet running across the floor, then up the steps, then down the hall, and then... the door bursts open and my children, Jabari and Kiri'Anna, running, jumping into my arms. "We missed you soooo much dad!" They exclaim in unison. "Soooo much!" I feel such warmth, such joy coming from them. They are my babies, they are my children when Jabari was about 4 and K.K. (as we called her) was about 2 years old. They fall about me the way puppies would with a child. All around me. I laugh, they laugh, we embrace.

But this cannot be real, I think to myself. They cannot be Here. This house predates them by 30 or 40 years. Is this some sort of subconscious wish fulfillment? A recapturing what I lost? I know this is a dream. I know this is not real. They are not with me. This is illusion.

Then the pain of the realization kicks in. I loosen my embrace. Kiri'Anna stops, frowns, "No, dad. No." Then Jabari says, "But we love you, dad, we love you sooo much!" They snuggle in close. They embrace me. I feel the sadness, it over comes me. "I love you too, but..." the words won't come. I can't make the words come. "Tickle Monster and Tackle Monster!" They exclaim. This dream, though I know it is a dream, is not fluid. I am not in control. We hold each other. Time freezes in this moment of combined extreme happiness and sorrow.

"Where is Khabira?" I ask them. At that moment, Kiri'anna lifts her face. There is such sadness in her eyes. She pushes away from me and slowly, nearly imperceptibly, fades from our presence. Jabari is now crying. He looks at me with such sadness, "But we love YOU, daddy," he says. Then just as KK did, he dissipates.

I look around searching for them. I call out to them. Nothing. The home is empty... with pain. It is suddenly no longer a home. It is something else. I move to the stairwell and walk downstairs. As I descend, the end of a couch comes into view. Then a little foot. A tiny foot. A baby's foot? The children? My anticipation grows.

I am surprised to find it is my son Tamars... as an infant. He looks over to me, and in a most adult and sophisticated voice, he says, "You don't get it dad, you just don't get it.

You have been given this great and wonderful gift, and you just don't get it."

"What do you mean?" I ask.

Jabari and KK. You don't get it dad.

You don't even know them, you never met them.

I don't have to meet them to know them. That's how things work out there. I know them Here. And you are hurting them.

Hurting them how?

They have been calling and trying to find you for many, many years, and when they finally find you, when they finally re-unite with THEIR father, you push them away.

"But," I say, "it isn't real. This is just a dream. Wish fulfillment. Trying to retain something I lost."

"They lost it too, dad," he says. "They lost just as much as you. And they have been looking for it, to get it back. This is real to them. The love, the happiness they lost. They found it again, and you have taken from them their only REAL chances of having it. You don't get it, dad. You just don't get it."

I exit the reality. Tears stream down my face.

Something Within Nothingness

I enter a reality suspended in what seems to be...nothing. At the instance of my awareness, however, it no longer is. Is is. And I am central. Yet, somehow, though it is, and I am central, it remains (my perception of it) nothing.

I move neither forward nor backward... nor any perceptible direction. Yet, I am in motion. Thought. Thought propels me. within Time? As Time? They are the only things not suspended Here in this non-somethingness; they are the only living things- thought... And time.

Time? As Life? It is the source of my self-declaration- that, at some moment, there was no I, and then, at some other moment, "I" became... Central. Suspended in non-somethingness. And I, being central, must define This; I must define This because I am the only one with the power to do so. Mines is the only thought Here.

This is reality. And as its definer, I own it. It is my reality. But, in awakening within this nothingness, am I illusion? The illusion I am a central thing within Nothing? What then of my reality? What does reality mean if this is true?

I exit that reality

Spiritual Connection

Figure 11 Spiritual connection

I am within a non-dominant reality, in the deep, rural south. South Carolina, I believe. I observe a disturbance. Some youths are angry. About something. Something that has to do with being treated unfairly. So, in their anger, they have taken to burning things. Buildings. On the "white side" of town. Now amidst the burning buildings, there is chaos as the white citizenry, now afraid and (themselves) angry, scamper throughout the streets of this small, rural, southern town. I observe it all. I walk in the midst of it all. No one can see me. They move right through me as they scamper around.

I watch a couple of black youths running toward the "black" section of town. They are caught by the police. They are wrestled to the ground and hand cuffed. Others of the group escape to the side of the "tracks" on which they were raised, which they know better than the white cops. I observe, slowly walking toward the black part of town.

I see a man, a black man, running towards me. I pay him little attention, other than to note he has a frantic look on his face. I prepare for him to move through me as I watch youths escape toward the black part of town. "Have you seen Kevin?" the man asks, his eyes on the verge of tearing. "Have you seen my son?"

"You can see me?" I ask, half surprised.

"Of course I can, idiot. Have you seen my son, Kevin?"

He reaches to brush me aside so he can move past me. When he does, everything changes. I am no longer a dispassionate observer. I am within the man. Though I am familiar with this, I am disoriented because it happened so fast and unexpectedly. I am in the man. I am still separate from him, but I can feel what he feels, see what he sees. Everything he experiences I experience. I am still me. I am familiar with this; it has happened before.

I, the man, continue walking toward the commotion and the burning buildings on the white side of town. Now I am familiar with this place. I have memories of it, its people. Through the man, I understand this place. I can feel his fear. It is strong. Suddenly, I, he… pauses. Near a vehicle. He sees rushing toward him four men… police. They have their batons and weapons drawn. He recognizes one of the men. They are friends. They play softball together. The man, I, relax… a little.

The men reach him. Three of them (but not his friend) slam him to the vehicle and hand cuff him. He makes eye contact with his friend. "I have nothing to do with this, Jerry, tell them I have nothing to do with this… I am looking for Kevin, Jerry, have you seen Kevin?" His "friend," Jerry does not acknowledge him. "You know this nigger, Jer?" one of the other cops asks. "No." replies Jerry. But he does. He does know the man. They play softball together- on the same team- a couple towns over. They are teammates, they are friends. His "friend," jerry,

39

denies him... doesn't acknowledge him. And the man, shaken to his core with fear, understands.

The police do not take him to the police station. They walk him back to the "black" part of town. They walk him back to his home. They know where he lives because his "friend" jerry knows. And jerry directs his fellow policemen to the man's home. They look for his son, Kevin. "We don't have nothing to do with this," the man begins to repeat to himself. Over and over. But no one acknowledges him. jerry doesn't acknowledge him.

They arrive at the man's home. jerry and another cop go inside to look for Kevin. A few seconds later, the other cop comes out of the home and joins the two with the man. They now surround him. One of the cops, his baton drawn, begins questioning the man: "where you been, nigger, where were you goin tonight?" He taps the man on his leg-near the right knee with the baton. The man knows, instinctively, epigenetically, to not respond. I feel his fear, his courage. I feel resolve swell within him. "Where you goin?" the cop asks again, hitting him, this time, harder on his leg... farther up from the knee. The other cops draw closer. The circle is tightening. "I asked you a question, nigger." The cop now gives the man a full blow to his groin... Pain. Fear. Courage. Resolve. "When we find your little nigger," one of the other cops says, "we gone hang both of you."

Courage. Resolve.

As the cops begin to beat him, he notices (and I feel) the cuffs were not tightened fully. They are loose. He feels he can slide them off if he can get them over his wrists. But he doesn't struggle, he doesn't make the beating worse. Suddenly, there is a scream. Anguish. He knows the voice to which it belongs. "Oh, god, no, god no!" the woman yells. He, I, can feel the depth of her sorrow and pain. "They done hung my boy. They done hung my Kevin!" she screams.

Just then, a child, a baby of maybe 1 or 2 years crawls out onto the porch of the house. jerry, the cop, the "friend," the softball teammate comes out and scoops up the baby. Following him is the woman to whom the screams belong… she is wailing now. The cop with the baton, who is beating the man along with the other two says, with an evil calmness that even now, as I write this, send chills through my being, "Hang them all. Hang every last one of them; then burn the house to the ground." I, the man, turn to the baton-wielding cop. I see through the cop. I see the beast within the cop. The creature who stood before me, who told a room full of whites how to kill me- how to kill us. I see The eyes. Those beautiful blue eyes. Those teeth. Menacing. I do not know if the man can see this beast. I do. And my rage, not his, boils. It intensifies. As it does, I feel a pushing. Something pushes me out of the man. I struggle to stay within him as my rage intensifies. As it does, it seems to push me out of the man. I no longer feel him. I only feel my rage. I am within him, being pushed out. My rage. I cannot contain it.

I am no longer within the man. I am outside. I observe from the outside… again. But it is different this time. Everything, everyone is frozen. Time has stopped. The three cops are frozen in their beating of the man. jerry is frozen grasping the infant. The infant. The infant is not frozen. It moves. Quivering. There is something within it. Something within...coming out. Exiting. MY GRANDFATHER??!!!

My grandfather leaves the infant's body. He was inside the infant, like I was inside the man?! I am confused. I don't understand this. I don't understand what is happening. I watch my grandfather leave the infant. I watch him ascend. "Pop," I call out to him. But he doesn't see me; he doesn't hear me. He looks down on us... at the infant. There is a look of extreme sadness in his eyes. His obsidian eyes. He has a look of understanding on his face. Of wisdom. Then, he is gone.

"Did you see him?" There is a hand on my shoulder. It is the man I was within. I turn to face him. "Did you see him?" he repeats.

"Yes, I saw him. It was my grandfather. I don't understand what's happening Here."

"Somehow," the man says, "he was connected to my infant. Like you are connected to me."

"I don't understand what's happening. This never happened before," I say.

The man takes a deep breath. Then says, "I don't fully understand it all. All I know is this night, me and my family died at the hands of these people. They hung my son, Kevin. This cop, who was my friend, jerry, he killed my infant boy this night. Snapped his neck right in front of me.

These two cops raped and killed my wife, and this one, this one with the baton, beat me to death. Then the mob burned our house down and dragged our bodies all over town. That happened tonight. This night. It happened, but no one knows or remembers because we were nobodies. We were nothing. But you and that man who was in my infant son...

Figure 12 My grandfather's spirit leaving the man's child.

did you see the woman too? Did you see the woman who was in my wife?"

"What woman?" I ask, "I saw no woman, I just saw my grandfather in the infant... and, and I saw that monster in that one cop."

"Monster? What monster? There was a woman in my wife like your grandfather was in my son and you were in me. They left, they went up. You stayed Here. You're still Here talking to me. Somehow, we are connected to y'all. Somehow y'all was Here for this... perhaps to remember."

"But my grandfather is dead. He can't remember?"

"You are wrong. He is not dead. I don't understand it fully, but nothing that is connected to other things ever dies. They remain... connected. Always. You are always connected to me... this moment... this event. Always. And your grandfather, and the woman who was in my wife."

"I don't understand," I said.

"I don't think you're supposed to understand. I don't think you're supposed to interpret. You're supposed to experience; remember so that we are never forgotten."

I exit that reality

The Fourth Dimension?

Figure 13 Dreams: the 4th dimension

I enter a reality observing the inter-dimensionality of my consciousness interacting with itself. I observe uniplanar consciousnesses create multi-dimensional Spacetime vis a vis this interaction. I observe myself- as product of my consciousness- interact with myself on multiple planes of existence and create new planes of existence.

I understand these interactions are processes, each process creating something different within its respective dimension. I observe dimensions concretize only when interactions synchronized. I understand this ephemerality is the essence of existence (physical and nonphysical).

What we call one, two, and three-dimensional existence is nothing more than different planes of consciousness

45

temporarily synchronizing within SpaceTime. And perhaps these are the various levels of brainwave patterns our machines observe and measure during sleep: testable, measurable, observable interactions and temporary synchronizations of varying planes of consciousness manifesting multidimensional levels of existence.

And Here, I perceive (or guess at through observation) a "fourth dimension" of SpaceTime: Dreaming.

And it comes full circle. The Serpent eats its tail. Gwnrt.w[20] in a sense. I think of my father. The time we spent together when he arrived and taught me about these Here's.

I exit that reality

---

[20] Psychospiritual principle of energy recycling.

Homecoming

I enter a reality being led by someone to a courtroom. As we enter, the person motions me to a seat. Placing their finger to their mouth, they signal I should remain quiet. I comply.

A judge is seated behind his bench. Before him several individuals are seated; they have name plates in front of them that read: Mary, Martin, Barry, William, Karen. There are others seated, scattered throughout the courtroom, but these are the only names I could make out (or recall?). I could not make out any faces.

The judge seems to be finishing a statement to all present when he says: "...Allow me to conclude this discussion before it begins. I need not confess any contemporary or historical religion to be a 'good' person. I need only decide to be a good person according to my sense of good. Confessing religion merely aligns one with like-minded individuals expressing similar interpretations of our places in reality. There is nothing metaphysical or spiritual about it. It is all psycho-social, ingroup/outgroup dynamic.

"Therefore, if one is adequately perspicacious, one observes of the overtly religious: the incantations and rituals serve to instill feelings of (exaggerated) favor from (highly psychopersonal, but nonetheless imagined) deities. They feel senses of moral loftiness that simply do not exist. They feel they possess knowledge of physical and metaphysical realities others cannot acquire (unless they convert); moreover, they feel a privy life (or lives) await them (after death) from which others will be exempt (unless, again, conversion). It is, in final analysis, a simple-minded twist on an old psychological defense mechanism-namely the Superiority Complex- which at its core becomes indistinguishable from other such psychological maladies; for example, racism (he looks at Barry and Martin), genderism or sexual orientation (he looks at Mary).

"We may conclude of the overtly religious: as with sufferers of similarly situated psychosocial maladies using pleasant demeanors, they attempt to conceal from the public otherwise fearful, hateful, lonely, socially and morally depraved inner selves."

He then turns toward me, gets up from his seat, and approaches me. As he does, reality fades. There is no more court room or people. There is just him. He stands before me and says,

"I am glad you accepted my invitation. I never really understood or accepted the ceremony of the '3 taps' to be real. But I guess it is because Here you are. I am your great, great, great grandson. I wanted you to witness this today because I needed you to know many of us, your descendants, found our way back to you. We found our way home."

He smiles. He holds out his hand to shake mine. I take his hand and shake it. He then, using the same hand, pounds his chest over his heart twice. I instinctively do the same.

Using the same hand, he makes a fist and holds it before me, stomach high. Again, instinctively, I make a fist, and bump his. At that point, he opens his hand, raises it above his head, and makes an explosion sound. I do the same. We both exclaim, "We are the same!"

He stares deeply into my eyes for a long time. He smiles. "You can now rest well as ymyw.h't, ole man." He fades, leaving behind only his smile.

I exit that reality

I simultaneously tear and smile with combinations of pride and joy.

They made it back home. They found me.

The Singular Consciousness

In a reality, I fall asleep watching the movie *__Everything, Everywhere, All at Once__*" (as it turns out, less than three minutes into the movie). I enter another reality seated in front of Michelle Yeoh.

Figure 14 Everything exists as everything within this consciousness.

She takes my hand in hers, she smiles, and says, "Come walk with me." We walk, and as we do, I notice all about us changes. The scenery, the people, us, our clothes. This does not confuse me because I have experienced it before. Ms. Yeoh smiles, she speaks:

"I met your mother once, you know, before everything began; I met her again- or should I say at the same time she fashioned your ⊔."

"You know my mother?" I asked.

She smiles that beautiful smile she beams when she understands something you have yet to understand, "You still haven't thought it all the way through yet, have you?"

"No ma'am," I say, "I think I've got some of it nailed down, but a lot of it is still a work in progress."

She stops, turns to me, and looks deeply into my eyes. "It will come. It will come. Just be prepared when it does."

She turns toward our direction of travel and continues walking. We talk for a long time, I feel, but I cannot remember the conversations. I just remember the people and scenery changing... like portals passing by us. I remember her stopping abruptly. She no longer smiled. She stared at me with what seemed to me a sense of urgency. Then she said:

"Within infinite being, every possible existence does- infinitely- and concurrently. Thus, I have existed, do exist, and will exist as every possible you- eternally. And you have existed, are existing, and will exist as every possible me. Everything exists as everything else has, does or will. We are one existence. What we experience as separateness is the ephemeral, multidimensional asynchronization of singular consciousness sequenced into illusions of beginnings and endings."

She then slowly faded. The scenery and people faded. I was left in the middle of what I can only describe as nothing that is simultaneously something. It seemed familiar, it all seemed so familiar.

I exit that reality. When I do, the credits are rolling. The name "Michelle Yeoh" scrolls across the screen.

It is becoming difficult to determine from which reality I write.

Molds & The Fourth Intermediate Period

Figure 15 How they built MrKB (pyramid).

I enter a nondominant reality. I observe as large numbers of men construct some sort of edifice. I maneuver to get a closer look, but Djhwty, who stands next to me, motions I remain still. "Your Rk[21], this moment, extends no further than this," it says.

So, I observe from a distance.

The men work together with a harmony bordering musical. They hum as they move. It reminds me of our ymyw.h't as they worked chain gangs, or railroads, or cotton fields, or anything requiring coordinated, rhythmed motions. And I understand, now, who molded our ymyw.h't; who placed within them that music, that harmony. They are magnificent. Beautiful.

I watch them construct what appear to be large moldings. I watch as they pour ground up substances into the molds and then mix in some kind of liquid. Water? The molds are gigantic and positioned precisely next to one another. (As my father and I had done many, many times when we constructed stone fixtures in our backyard on Diamond Street; as he had done many times when he constructed

---

[21] Knowledge

driveways and fences). There had to be thousands of molds and perhaps 10 times as many men. Measuring, checking and double checking and checking again. Craftsman. Master Craftsmen.

I watch until they construct what appears to be a four cornered base. A precise square. Enormous.

I watch as R.w- in its Sr.w aspect- descends below the Western Horizontal Plane, and Sr.t ascends the night sky to remember, seek, and show the lost the way to Dwt.

The men, simultaneously, descend into sleep. And I understand. I understand who these men are. These great men, Gwnstr.w, whose names have returned to Rt.w. Those who left within their magnificent structures all memory of who they were. Who we are destined to become... Again.

I watch them repeat this circadian-like rhythm over the course of decades. I watch them complete the edifice. And I understand. They did not carry or drag. They made the boulders on site. They fit them into place not as finished product, but as easily positioned skeletons. Then, before the boulders dried, they used simple tools and scraped- to precision- the spaces between those monoliths. I watch them build the "inner chambers" as the boulders finish drying around them, making scraping adjustments as needed. I watch them work their way to the apex of their monumental achievement and crown it with a miniature version of the whole. Gold tipped.

I turn to Djhwty with tear filled eyes. "This is how it was done," it says to me, as it records in Rk M Kfw. "This is how it was done," I whisper solemnly. I kneel there, before ymyw.h't. I kneel in remembrance. I lower my head to honor them. All of them.

Djhwty reads to those who comprehend:

"NHS AND Y.DY FROM SDG SONS AND DAUGHTERS OF THE LAST MWT N NSW.BJT. UNDERSTAND THE NATURE OF MOLDS. THEY SYMBOLIZE KM.T IS NOT YET COMPLETE. THIS IS INTERMEDIATE- THE FOURTH IN DJFD.YRY'S STORY, WHICH IS CLOSED WHILE SHE NAVIGATES THE TWELVE GATES.

"WHEN SHE COMPLETES THE PHASES OF ASCENSION AND WBNW KHT, THE CHILDREN OF P'T NN.W P'T WILL EXIT YMHT, WBN, AND COMMENCE WPT-RNT M KHT. UNTIL THEN, STUDY, TRAIN, AND PREPARE FOR THE MOMENT DJFD.YRY OPENS AND MWT N NSW.BJT RETURNS IN HER ASPECT AS T'NTR."

Djhwty closes Rk M Kfw.

Figure 16: MrKB construction

That Cat

I am within a nondominant reality. I seem to be in some type of container (a box?) in which there are several levers and other gadgets. There's a cat(?) in here too. A Tabby it seems to me... or a Cheshire-it grins. It's perched on a ledge, its tail dangling over the side-twitching (it seems to me) nervously, uncontrollably. It stares at me as though I am a mouse... or dinner that has arrived annoyingly late. I initiate this conversation:

What is this?

It is a box; I think I- and now you- take part in some sort of experiment.

An experiment? What sort of experiment?

I can't be sure. But everything seems symbolic.

Symbolizing what? To what end?

I cannot say for sure, but I think it has something to do with whether I am alive, or dead, or both at the same time. (The Cat directs my attention to one side of the box.) Do you see that over there?

Yes.

Well, I think it is a vial- some type of poison. I think the idea is the poison has either killed me or it has not. Or it has simultaneously killed and not killed me.

Killed you?! You mean killed US! I am here too!

Yes, there's that.

How long have you been here? How do we get out of here?

As for the first, how long have you been here? And to the second, we don't.

I cannot say with any certainty how long I have been here; when I opened my eyes just now, I was here. And what do you mean we don't get out of here? Of course, we do. We leave. Where is the exit?

How does one, as component of a thought, exit the thought?

Thought? Cat, you are speaking in riddles.

Which is what we are within, my friend.

We are within a riddle?

No, a thought, which is the riddle.

The thought is the riddle?

Is it not, sir, in terms of its existence, just that? And would not any component of it be so trapped- wound within it, constituent and just as enigmatic? For does not asking, "What is a thought?" existentially and beyond consciousness, question the nature of existence itself? I have had time to consider this question, and it is the conclusion at which I arrive over and over.

You are very smart and well-spoken for a "cat."

I have been here, sir, with nothing but thought at my disposal. Can you fathom such an existence?

How long have you been here?

It is difficult to say without any understanding beyond "here," but I think I first appeared in 1935.

1935! It is now 2023. Are you telling me you have been here for 88 years?

It would seem so, if your determination of time is correct. The alternative- it is 1935, which would present for you an interesting feat of physics if you first appeared from 2023.

Who placed you here? What twisted, perverted mind conceived of concealing a cat in a box for 88 years?

Who? I cannot say for sure, but I think he was an Austrian fellow. And as far as my confinement, I don't think he knows or knew I remained here once he moved on. I don't think he realized others came along to perpetuate the matter.

What do you mean? Are you saying others have come along and kept you here instead of releasing you?

In a manner of speech, yes.

Why?

I don't think people understand the nature of my existence here. It is sort of like, what you may call an "Escape Room." You cannot leave until you solve the puzzle or puzzles constituent to it- or in this case, the box.

So, you cannot leave until someone solves the puzzle of this box?

Just so, sir.

And so, no one has come in to solve this puzzle and release you?

I don't think anyone has thought to "come into" the box, sir.

How can they possibly solve the puzzle from the outside?

Just so, sir. Hence, my confinement.

That is terrible. Like a sentence for crimes you did not commit.

Just so, sir. But something occurred to me recently.

What is that?

Well, it occurred to me: if my existence is an experiment in thought requiring solution to a puzzle, and the solution resides within the thought itself, why could I not create a thought, place it here with me, and urge it to solve the puzzle?

That is complex thinking, but also, it seems to me, possibly accurate. Did you attempt it? What happened if you did?

I did not attempt it until this very moment, so I will have to let you know how it goes.

What do you mean, "until this very moment?"

You, sir, I mean you.

What do you mean me? I am not a thought. Certainly not your thought.

You now sound like a man named Odjko.

Who is that?

He is a man quite famous is these realms for his insistence on existing as he did not exist.

I am not anything like this Odjko, I exist.

Just so, sir, but can you tell me how you arrived here?

This is a nondominant reality I have entered.

Whose reality? Yours?

No, not mines. I am asleep at this moment.

Well, sir, if you are asleep somewhere, that is a physical locality determination. You are physically there and here also?

I cannot say for certain, but I am not actually physically here. This is some sort of conscious rendering.

Whose consciousness, sir, yours?

To the extent my consciousness interacts within this SpaceTime.

Indeed, sir, but what does that say of me? By your own definition, this is MY reality. To the extent MY consciousness interacts within this SpaceTime and creates This. You, sir, therefore, must be a part of my reality since when you arrived here, I was already present. Would this not be true? Would it not be true you are an aspect of MY consciousness interacting within this SpaceTime in which you inexplicably find yourself?

Cat, you are clever, but...

Yes, I know, you are going to tell me you have a life, you have a daughter, you have an existence separate from me.

Yes, I do. All of that is true.

How could I, a mere cat, know this. How could I know what you are about to say, sir? Moreover, how could I know everything you have said, or will ever say? Think about it logically, sir, a cat? With all of this knowledge?

You do not, you could not possibly.

But I do. Everything about you I know. Because you are my thought. You exist as part of my consciousness.

IMPOSSIBLE!!!

Okay, your name is Kf.w M Kht- it's not really, but let's leave it there. You have a daughter whom you are raising alone. She is currently an honor student, who is excited about entering high school; she's not sure what she wants to be, but she is excited about the journey toward discovery. You live in...

STOP! This is insanity!

Just so, sir, from your perspective. And I cannot say I blame you for your confusion. You must understand, however, and I believe you were warned about this several times, none of this is within you. It, I, everything exists beyond you. Beyond your consciousness. I have learned, during my time of confinement, great care must be taken when consciousness is involved. Because there are no boundaries here. Consciousnesses intersect and interact- sometime benevolently, sometimes not. I could go on, but this is digression. This is not the argument; you have a different purpose for being Here.

And so, cat, what is it? What is my reason for being here.

If I were to joke, and therefore nail proverbial coffins shut, I would say your reason for being is to become more than thought stuff; but let me resist such sarcasms. Sir, you are here to solve the puzzle.

Which will set you free?

In a manner of speaking. Not true freedom, but freedom from this box in any case. So, the question to you is this: how is it that not knowing which exists of an "either-or" proposition renders both possibilities true simultaneously?

Not knowing, cat, would not make that case. Not knowing would only place one in a state of ignorance, which has no bearing on the truth.

Explain, sir.

Take this box, in which you have been confined for so long, and that vial of poison. If outside of this box, someone lacks knowledge of its interior reality- that is whether you are alive or dead- that ignorance has no bearing on the truth within the box. There is no connection between the two beyond not knowing. For the ignorant, whether you are alive or dead is an unknown only. That "not-knowing" cannot possibly render you both dead and alive.

How is that sir?

Because YOU, cat, know whether you are alive or dead. You KNOW you are not both. And no one outside the box can alter your reality simply because they don't know it.

Just so. Just so, sir. However, it occurs to me there is another consideration.

And that would be?

There is the question, beyond knowledge, of consciousness.

How is that cat?

Let us return, sir, for a moment, to your current circumstance. You said earlier, you are asleep somewhere. That suggests to me one of two things: 1) you are physically somewhere other than here, and you are simultaneously physically here, in this box, with me. or 2) you are NOT in fact physically here with me, and it is just your consciousness that is here while you are physically asleep someplace else. And one of those, sir, must be the truth.

That would seem so.

This circumstance of yours is of particular interest to me, sir, because I in fact believe you are a product of my mind. A thought. Which is to say, your consciousness is not currently your own; rather it is an aspect of mine.

A matter about which, cat, I completely disagree.

Just so, sir. So, I hope you can appreciate my dilemma, which is to say, at this moment, you are either an aspect of MY consciousness or you are, in fact consciously here and separate from me.

Which I am.

We, sir, find ourselves puzzles within a puzzle. Because if you are consciously here with me AND where you are asleep, then there is something to be said for the experiment of this box.

How so, cat?

Well, sir, you are both there AND here at this very moment. That would mean, independent of external knowledge of which, it is possible we are both. You are both here and there, and I am both alive and dead. Those are our realities.

But, cat, I am here with you, you are not dead AND alive. You are not both.

Just so, sir, but you are here with me now, and I could say you could not possibly be here and somewhere asleep; yet, you are adamant that is the truth! So, it seems to me either I am right, and you are an aspect of my consciousness- a thought- or you are right, and you are your own consciousness. Or it is possible you are both.

I cannot deny the logic.

Just so, sir. But if you are your own entity possessing a consciousness independent of mine, that changes the dynamic of this interaction.

How so, cat?

In just this way: if you are not an aspect of my consciousness, that means I am not now suffering from some form of crisis of consciousness due to my confinement. However, I am convinced you are an aspect of my consciousness. So, the question becomes: how do we put the matter to test and arrive at a definitive answer?

It is simple, cat. I will at some point awaken from this.

Just, so. Or, sir, you will not.

Through the entirety of our discussion, that cat maintained the most sinister of grins. When I had achieved what it apparently desired of me, it slowly moved, from where it was perched, toward me. It moved deliberately, as a tiger stalking its prey. It walked over to me and sat on its hind legs. Its smile, at this distance, seemed more like a sneer. "I owe you the greatest of debts, sir," it said, "and I am most remorseful that I must ask of you one more thing before I leave what has been my prison for so long." It paused, as though in deep thought. Then it opened its mouth wide, revealing teeth that were like blades. That cat leaned in, its mouth bearing down, preparing to devour me, and asked:

Figure 17: That Cat!

You are the Truth Within
Questions Not Yet Imagined

I enter this reality. In it, i am sleep. I am aware of this sleep, but not in the sense I am aware i sleep in my predominant reality; I am only aware of myself as dream me sleeping. Dream me doesn't seem to have any awareness of Me.

he begins to awaken, and from a distance, he hears a female's voice. "There you are sleepy head," she says, "I thought you would never make it. They told me it sometimes takes a while for you to come around. I- they said- have to be patient."

he is confused.

The woman walks towards him as he rises to a seated position. She takes a seat in a chair next to the bed. She stares, almost lovingly, as he gathers consciousness.

"Who are you? Where am I," he asks.

"I am, from certain points of view, your 3rd level great granddaughter"

"My great granddaughter? That's impossible. I don't have children."

"Not your great granddaughter, my love. Your 3rd level great granddaughter."

At that moment, she turned to look at me. Up to that point, I thought I was dream observing them, taking an outside perspective of me (for whatever reason). There, but not there in the sense anyone could see Me. But she could, and she motioned for Me to both be quiet and sit next to her. A chair that had not previously been there materialized as she did.

I walk over and sit next to her. Now I am confused also. I begin to speak, but she motions I should remain silent. I gesture to speak anyway, but before I could utter a sound, she said:

"You must remain quiet, or you will confuse him. Though he is not aware of and separate from you, from his perspective, your thoughts are not separate, and if you are not careful, you will confuse him, make him think he is insane."

"What?" he questions.

Turning her attention back to him, she says, "Nothing, love. There was a nuisance trying to come between us."

"Okay, who are you again?"

"I told you, your 3rd level great granddaughter."

"But not my great granddaughter?"

"No. You don't have a great granddaughter, as you pointed out. You don't have any children."

"How, HOW is that possible?"

She takes a deep breath, she sighs. "Let's see, how can I best explain this to you." When she says this, she looks at me and places her hand on my knee, letting me know what follows is for Me and me.

"You understand geometry, yes?" She asks.

"I do. I am a mathematician, after all," he replies.

(A mathematician? I HATE math, I think to myself).

She gives me a sharp, quick, disturbing look, as though she understood my thoughts.

"I'm a mathematician, but I hate math?" he questions.

"No, sweetie, you love math. You are a mathematician," she continues, "let's take a geometrical point. A dot…"

She abruptly stops. She looks at him intently. "SHIT!," she shouts. "Losing him," she mutters disappointingly to herself. "He's going."

I turn to watch me slowly fade. he looks at her confused. "What's happening? Why are you fading"?

"I'm not dear heart, you are. You have rejected this reality due to a logical contradiction. You are waking up."

I turn to her. She looks at me and smiles broadly. "But you are making strides. You are coming around."

"Who are you- WHO IS THAT? Where did that dude come from?" He questioningly shouts, pointing.

She turns quickly to him, then to Me. She points at Me and attempts to explain, "oh, he, he is…"

"What are you pointing at" he says to her. "Who is that?" he points past us to a corner in the room. There is nothing there that we can see. He fades completely.

At that moment, she begins to fade. I understand what's happening. I understand all too well.

"Wait!" I shout, "I still don't get the levels thing."

Still smiling, she says softly:

"Open your mind. Accept This reality. Accept that everything, everyone Here is real. Not dream concoctions. Also, it may help if you start thinking in geometric dimensions. Like a cube within a cube within a cube…except the number of cubes is infinite.

"And imagine, within each cube there are near infinite amounts of thin membranes[22]- let's call them branes for short; and let us say, for the sake of understanding, there are as many branes within each cube as there are galaxies within your observable universe; and on each brane there are as many universes as there are atoms in your body.

"Now imagine the cubes, branes, and universes are all in motion about one another. That is to say the cubes move about one another, as do the branes within the cubes, as do the universes within the branes. And imagine that, at times, during their movements, they collide, or merge

---

[22] The concept of multidimensional "branes" was developed during the 1980's & '90's by notable physicists and mathematicians such as: Michael Duff, Joseph Polchinski, Edward Witten, Paul Townsend, and Cumrun Vafa.

with, or pass through one another- all of these moving parts."

She pauses. She inspects me quietly. "Are you picturing it?" she says.

"Yes," I reply. "It is a lot to take in, but I see it. I see it all."

"Very, very good. You understanding this is important to what comes next," She continues, "Now, every cube is a level of consciousness; and each brane within each cube is a level of consciousness, and every universe on each brane is a level of consciousness."

"They represent consciousness?" I interrupt.

"No," she replies, "They are consciousness. Separate, but interrelated consciousness." She pauses. She stares at me intently to determine if she has lost me- if she has reached the point where my intelligence can go no further.

I frown, trying to grasp the concept of it all. "Wait, soooo, they are all... Wait, sooo, is it one consciousness? Or many?"

She smiles as though she is happy I am on track with her explanation. "One, with many aspects and levels," she replies.

"So..." I try to continue her logic- to take it to a conclusion of sorts, "so everything is an aspect of a singular consciousness. All interrelated and interacting with one another?"

"YES!!!" She exclaims. I nod that I understand this insane improbability. But I at the same time accept it all as fact.

With a large smile, she continues:

"Consider your body. All your cells, though separate, are integrated. They are all aspects of you. All interrelated aspects of the whole. That's what This is. That's what all of This is. That's us. Whatever This consciousness is, we are aspects of it. Separate within ourselves, but interrelated and integrated aspects. And just like the cells of your body, in the aggregate add up to you, we, in the aggregate are This... consciousness."

"So," I say after a few moments' reflection, "are we then like the nerves of this consciousness?"

"No. Go deeper. We are more like the impulses flowing through the nerves. We are quanta. We are the smallest possible, meaningful units of this consciousness. We are the threshold, beyond which, this consciousness has no substantial meaning, identity, or reality. The same is true of us," she continues, "There are thresholds, beyond which, we lose all substantial meaning, identity, or reality. Perhaps it is within our cells; perhaps it is within whatever resides within that. At some point, the deeper we go, we come upon a place, a reality within which we no longer possess an 'I.'"[23]

"So, this consciousness, is it aware of us?"

"I believe," she replies, "no more than you are aware of the impulses driving your consciousness."

---

[23] I have also come to realize at some point within higher dimensional realities, we no longer possess substantial meaning or identity. This, it seems, preserves conscious integrity and continuity.

71

"So, then, how is it, or why is it that we interact Here? What function does it serve?"

"I believe, based on all my travels and experiences, this is a byproduct of its existence-an unintended consequence of its conscious processes."

"You mean to say it does not, it has no control over what happens Here? Our interactions and experiences Here?"

"Just so." she says, and an involuntary shiver of anxiety courses through my body. A sense of fear- not over what her words mean, but the words themselves. I try, but I cannot shake images of ferocious and clever cats. "Do not call me 'sir'" I mumble under my breath. "What?"

I ignore her. "So, how is it that we DO interact here?" I question, both changing the subject and returning to our original line of discussion.

"The movements of the cubes, branes, and universes facilitate our interactions. We interact within one another as they interact with one another. It all has to do with 'tethering, entanglement, and frequencies.'"

"Tethering entanglement, and frequencies?" I inquire, "I don't understand."

She takes a deep, sustained breath. She continues:

"As consciousness, we are tethered. We- I, and I believe you- are tethered to some kind of being. We are tethered to being for the duration of its existence as physical being. The relationship we have to being is complex.

"We are not the being, though, as consciousness, and tethered to it, we belong to it. But it does not own us. It is more like a renting or borrowing situation. Being kind of borrows us. Why this relationship exists, I cannot say, but it seems, based on my experiences and conversations I have had with others Here, physical being requires consciousness in order to attain measures of meaning. Without consciousness, being, while it may exist, has no substantial meaning.

"It seems consciousness confers upon physical being the ability to become aware- of itself and other physical beings. Once it achieves awareness, being and the consciousness it has acquired to achieve its awareness, are tethered for the duration of being's physicality."

"So then," I ask, "what are we outside of being. What are we as consciousness without being's physicality?"

"THAT!" she exclaims, "is perhaps the most fundamental question within ALL of This!" She places herself in deep thought. Then she speaks:

"Physical being provides for us identity. Until we tether to physicality, we exist without an identity because we are singular. A singular consciousness. No division, no compartments- singular. Within a reality, within an existence such as that, there is no 'I,' no 'me,' no 'us,' no 'them, they,' no any of that. There isn't even a 'we' because in order for any of those identities to exist, there has to be separation.

"Physicality- when we tether to physical being, we obtain an identity. It is highly complex and..."

At that moment she pauses. She slowly turns her head toward the area of the room i had pointed before he faded.

"COM----PLI---CATE---DED- Do you see that?" She abruptly says without looking at me.

"See what?" I say, looking at the area of the room she's now looking.

"That," she says as she slowly gets up and walks over toward a wall. "That right there, you don't see that?"

"No," I reply. "What do you see?"

"It's…it's You and…you?" She says questioningly, as though she can't believe it. Or… "This can't be possible. It's, it's…"

"It's what?" I say becoming more and more curious.

"It's me," she says. "Not Me, not the Me right Here right now. It's me, the me who should be asleep right now. How? How is this possible?"

She's now standing and staring at what to me is an empty wall. She is mesmerized, transfixed. She turns back and looks at me. She is completely puzzled. "What Ntr are you?"

I try to respond, but I can't. "I, I, I don't…"

She turns back to the wall. She slowly lifts her hand as though she reaches for something, or she attempts to touch something. Her index finger slowly inches forward. She is hesitant. To me she seems almost afraid. "How can that be me?" She says as her finger makes contact with the wall.

As soon as she touches the wall, there is a blinding burst of light. She is flung- or hurled- through the air. She impacts a wall on the other side of this room with such force, I am sure she was killed. She crumbles onto the bed beside which she had been speaking with me. She moans in agony. She attempts to get up. She stumbles. I take two steps toward her. "Are you okay?" I ask as I reach to grab her, to help her up.

"DON'T TOUCH ME!" she yells. There was fear in her voice. "You cannot touch me!" I step back. "Are you okay?" I ask again. "What happened? What was that light? What flung you across the room like that?"

Still moaning slightly, she gathers herself. She stands. She inspects her body. It seemed to me at first, she inspected to determine if she was harmed- if she had any broken bones, but as I watched her, I realized it was something else. She wasn't inspecting herself; she was inspecting... Everything? She looked at herself, at the room, as though she no longer knew who or where she was. "It is all so beautiful! I never imagined..." she says. Then she looks at me. Her eyes... Obsidian.

She stares at me for a long time. Questioningly. As though she attempts to understand. Me? As though I am a puzzle- or a piece to a puzzle she didn't even know she was trying to solve. At some point she smiled slightly.

"Are you okay?" I ask. She doesn't respond. She just stares at me. Tears began streaming down her face. She begins to tremble. Then suddenly she is calm; as though she has found an answer- THE answer- she was seeking.

She speaks:

"Everything you think you know about anything, you don't. Time, Space, Consciousness, they are not what you think. You don't know them. You never will. You can't."

"No, no!" I shout, "Don't fade away! What just happened? What did you see? What DO you see?"

Very calmly, very reassuringly, she says, "I am not fading, dear, You are." She pauses, smiles slightly then says, "You are the truth within questions not yet imagined."

She- I fade. The last I see... her obsidian eyes.

Everything around Me slowly fades and transitions to my room. Slightly disoriented, I look around. I see me tucked and soundly sleeping as my mother left him. Peaceful. I sit next to and look down on him:

"I now understand you... Us. I understand this relationship- why- how it exists. We are mutually, symbiotically tethered, each offering something the other cannot attain.

"I give you meaning and purpose. Through Me, you acquire memories of a past and desires for a future; a yearning for life; something to look back on; something to look forward to. Through Me you travel to worlds, encounter beings, and have experiences laying so far beyond your grasp, you could never imagine the possibilities. Without Me, just as you lay here now, you would exist in a perpetual state of unknowing. you would lack awareness… of anything. Though you would possess a self, it would be as alien to you as movement to an akinetic catatonic.[24] your existence would be that of a rock, or a mound of dirt. I connect you to The Singular, Omniversal Source Consciousness. I am everything eternal about you; I am that which will persist long after you have returned to dust; I am your ⊔.

"Through you I experience identity and selfness. Without you I am amorphous; I lack individuality. I have no experiences of my own. Without you, I am singular consciousness. Omnitemporaspatial- everywhere and nowhen simultaneously. Without you I have no certainty I am real, that I exist. I tether to you tightly because selfless existence is a death sentence; experiencing everything without the ability to claim anything. you provide me- in a sense- ownership of experience. Tethering to you is a pardon from the hell of anonymity."

I stare at him as I feel Myself fading into inevitabilities I cannot yet fathom.

The dream ends.

i awaken

---

[24] Disorder involving lack of movement.

Figure 18 Interacting cubes. Each cube is a megaverse.

Figure 19 Sliding branes. Each brane is a multiverse.

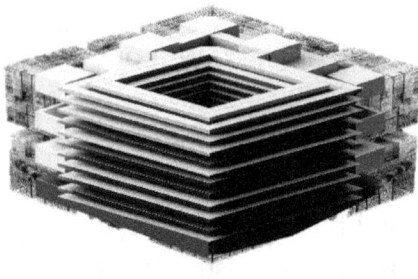

Figure 20 Branes interacting within cubes.

Figure 21 Megaverse cubes and Multiverse branes

Figure 22 Multiverse brane. Each dot is a universe.

Figure 23 Mega verse cubes within Omniverse consciousness

COMPILATIONS

FIGURES AND ILLUSTRATIONS

TERMS AND PHRASES

FRONT COVER

From top to bottom:

1.) Eintou- Black Pearl signifying Obsidian Eye and representing the corpus of Ancestral historico-cultural philosophies.
2.) Gwnrt.w- Principle of eternal energetic recycling.
3.) Mdw M Gwnstr- Words of the Ancestors meaning "awakenings."
4.) Adinkra symbol for "god."
5.) Mdw Ntr for "truth."
6.) Mdw M Gwnstr transliterated "everything is symbol" (read right to left).
7.) Tkn- Kmty.w symbol signifying the emergence of consciousness from nonconsciousness.
8.) HrmKht & Kns.w- the sphinx and moon.
9.) Kfw the EverBecoming in its aspect as a man.

BACK COVER

From top to bottom:

1) Omniversal Consciousness
2) Eintou as "third eye" symbolism
3) Obsidian Eyes signifying the ability to see, via ancestral historico-cultural reference, what cannot be seen and the enhanced consciousness commensurate with it.
4) Nhk- Kmtyw symbol for the energy that binds all life.

Contact Kfw M Kht:

414-807-6534
Facebook: Kfw M Kht
YouTube: Kfw Kht

www.ingramcontent.com/pod-product-compliance
Lightning Source LLC
Chambersburg PA
CBHW072041170626
46811CB00008B/3123